Natasha's Big Adventure

by Linda Cernak
illustrated by Jim Gordon

Harcourt
SCHOOL PUBLISHERS

Printed in China

ISBN 10: 0-15-351538-4
ISBN 13: 978-0-15-351538-5

Ordering Options
ISBN 10: 0-15-351214-8 (Grade 4 Advanced Collection)
ISBN 13: 978-0-15-351214-8 (Grade 4 Advanced Collection)
ISBN 10: 0-15-358128-X (package of 5)
ISBN 13: 978-0-15-358128-1 (package of 5)

4 5 6 7 8 9 10 0940 12 11 10 09

Natasha the cat spent most of her day lying about in the sun, washing her paws or snoozing. Jenny, the young girl with whom Natasha lived, thought Natasha was a very lazy cat.

"What an easy life you have, Natasha," said Jenny, scratching the cat under her neck. Natasha purred and rolled over, allowing Jenny to rub her belly.

It was time for bed, so Jenny gave Natasha a little snack. Natasha gobbled up her food quickly. "Cat food again," she thought. "I could really use a little variety. I'll just wait until Jenny goes to sleep. It's a perfect night to go scrounging around the neighborhood to find some good leftovers."

Jenny turned out the light, fidgeted a bit, and then snuggled deep under the covers. Natasha curled up on her little chair next to the bed and waited until Jenny was asleep. Then Natasha yawned casually and stretched in case Jenny wasn't really asleep. When Jenny didn't react, Natasha thought, "Time to rock and roll." Then she was off.

She padded quietly through the house to the kitchen, slipped through her cat door, and out into the night. Passing several neighbors' trash cans, she briefly checked them for leftovers. "Tonight's selection is pathetic," she thought. "People are being quite stingy with their leftovers. I think I'll head to the other side of town."

4

Natasha slipped through the streets and down the alleyways. She checked out the trash cans at the back of Vinny's Pizza. Vinny, the owner, always left some meatballs out for the cats in the neighborhood. Natasha licked her lips, ate the meatballs, and continued on her way.

By and by, she came to a warehouse near the docks. With a belly full of meatballs, Natasha began to feel a little sleepy. "Time for a little catnap," she thought as she slipped into the warehouse and scouted around for a cozy place to sleep. There were crates piled all over the place, and one crate was slightly open. Looking inside, Natasha saw several boxes cushioned with some shredded paper.

"What a perfect place for a nap," Natasha thought as she settled down and went to sleep.

With the first rays of sunlight, workers began their day at the warehouse. Today a shipment of crates needed to be loaded onto a truck. One by one, the workers used lifting machines to place the crates on the back of a truck. Natasha slept soundly as her crate was loaded.

"Okay, boys, that's the last one, so close them up," shouted Max, the foreperson. With that, the doors of the truck snapped shut, and the truck made its way out of the lot. Natasha still slept soundly inside her crate as the truck made its way onto the highway and headed for the airport.

At the airport, workers unloaded the crates, one by one, and placed them on an airplane. About seven hours later, the plane landed, trucks were backed up to the plane, and the crates were all unloaded. Natasha stirred a little in her sleep and stretched a bit, but still she did not wake up. The crates were loaded onto a truck, and then they were taken to another warehouse in a strange city. At the warehouse, workers took the crates off the truck. Then, upon finishing the day's work, the workers all went home.

Natasha opened her eyes. "What a good nap," she thought. She wiggled her way out of the crate and looked around. There was definitely something very different about the warehouse. Natasha became suspicious and wondered where she was.

Suddenly, she heard a noise. Crouching down, she peeked around the edge of the crate. There was another cat washing his paws.

"Hey, pssst," said Natasha.

"Who are you?" he asked.

"My name is Natasha," she said. "Where am I?"

"Why, my goodness, you are in a warehouse in the glorious city of London!" said Winston the cat.

"How far is that from New York?" she asked.

"Why, London is on the other side of the ocean," Winston answered. "Are you from New York, my dear?"

"Yes, but I don't know how I got here," said Natasha. "I was just taking a nap in this crate, and now here I am!"

"Well, that explains it," said Winston. "Those crates were just shipped in today from our warehouse in New York."

"What will I do?" sighed Natasha forlornly.

Winston looked at Natasha sympathetically. "Well, everyone is gone for the day, so there is not much we can do right now," said Winston. "I suggest we go out on the town. London is a lovely city all lit up at night!"

Natasha agreed, so off she and Winston went into the night. First, they went to the station to get on the "Tube," which is what London's subway is called. The new friends hopped aboard a train unnoticed. "Next stop, Piccadilly Circus!" shouted Winston. "Perhaps we can catch a show."

"What is Piccadilly Circus?" asked Natasha.

"Oh, it is a very lively part of our city. There are shows and restaurants and lights!" said Winston, his green eyes glowing.

Natasha and her new friend Winston got off at the stop for Piccadilly. They slipped through the streets and to the back of a restaurant. "The Indian food here is divine," said Winston. "I especially like the lamb curry. My friend Landi always leaves me leftovers from the restaurant."

"Sounds like my friend Vinny," said Natasha as they ate from a plate of food. "You're right, this is quite yummy." Bellies full, it was now time to take in the sights of the city.

"Shall we go and see Big Ben?" said Winston.

"Who is Big Ben?" asked Natasha.

"Not who, but what. Big Ben is the name of a very large clock bell inside one of the largest clock towers in the world," answered Winston.

The two cats made their way down London's famous Whitehall Street to Big Ben. As luck would have it, they got to the famous clock just at the stroke of midnight. The wonderful deep chimes of the clock sounded throughout London.

"How lovely," sighed Natasha.

"Would you like to see Westminster Abbey?" asked Winston. "It is a church where many of the kings and queens of England are buried. It is quite a noble sight to see."

"I just love stories about kings and queens," said Natasha. The two cats went over to the Abbey and slipped in through a secret passageway that Winston knew about. Inside, Natasha's green eyes glowed as she looked at the high ceiling and the lovely carved statues.

The next stop was the famous Tower of London where some of the crown jewels of the kings and queens of England are kept on display.

"Oh, Winston," she said, "I could see myself wearing such a fine crown."

"I do say, I think this one here would be the right match for you," said Winston, pointing to a lovely diamond crown.

As the cats made their way out of the tower, the sun began to shine. It was time to go back to the warehouse. They hopped on the "Tube" once again and rode the train back to the warehouse.

"Winston, it was a pleasure to spend the night out on the town with you, but I really must figure out how to get home," Natasha said with resolve.

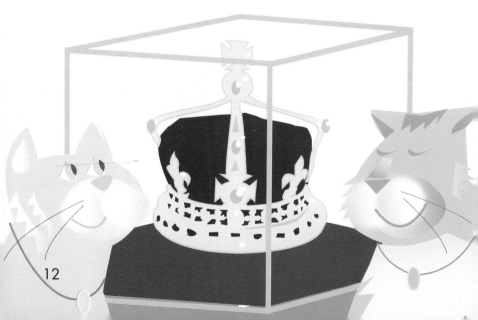

At the warehouse, Winston and Natasha ran into Charles, the owner of the warehouse. When Charles bent down to pet Natasha, he noticed the ID tag on her collar. "You've come all the way from New York! But how?"

Then he spotted the crate in which Natasha had made her long trip "Why, you must have been shipped with that crate! I noticed that the crate was open, and I wondered about it. Don't worry, kitty, I'll find you a way to get home."

Charles made a phone call to the airline that had shipped the crates. Before long, an airline worker pulled up to the warehouse in a car.

Winston peered out a warehouse window and said, "I think your ride home is here."

Natasha put her paw out to Winston. "You must come to visit me in New York."

"Maybe on the next shipment out," said Winston. "Good-bye, my friend!"

The airline worker put Natasha in a carrier and took her to the airport. The people at the airline had called Natasha's owners to tell them that they were flying her home. The worker gave the cat carrier to the flight attendant, who took her aboard the plane.

About seven hours later, the plane landed in New York. Jenny was waiting with her family in the baggage claim area. A flight attendant carrying Natasha in the cat carrier soon appeared.

"Oh Natasha, we were so worried about you!" said Jenny as she gave her cat a big hug.

Natasha purred because she was so glad to be home, but she would never forget her night out in the city of London with Winston the cat.

Think Critically

1. How would you describe Natasha the cat?

2. Tell the events in order that led up to Natasha ending up on a plane to London.

3. How did Winston help Natasha?

4. What other fantasy stories have you read? How are they like this story?

5. What was your favorite part of this story? Why?

Math

Figure it Out It is 3,470 miles (5,584 km) from New York to London. If it took Natasha seven hours to fly there, how fast did the plane travel?

School-Home Connection Share this story with a family member. Retell the story in your own words, acting out the parts of Natasha and Winston the cats.